For Jamie and his "sweet teeth"—M. P.

For Keek and Lucy—J. E. D.

SIMON & SCHUSTER BOOKS FOR YOUNG READERS
An imprint of Simon & Schuster Children's Publishing Division
1230 Avenue of the Americas, New York, New York 10020
Text copyright © 2004 by Margie Palatini
Illustrations copyright © 2004 by Jack E. Davis
All rights reserved, including the right of reproduction in whole or in part in any form.
SIMON & SCHUSTER BOOKS FOR YOUNG READERS is a trademark of Simon & Schuster, Inc.
Book design by Mark Siegel
The text for this book is set in Utopia.
The illustrations for this book are rendered in mixed media.
Manufactured in China
10 9 8 7 6 5 4 3 2 1
Library of Congress Cataloging-in-Publication Data
Palatini, Margie.
Sweet tooth / Margie Palatini ; illustrated by Jack E. Davis.
p. cm.
Summary: Stewart's loud, obnoxious sweet tooth constantly gets him into
trouble, until Stewart uses a healthy diet to take control of the
situation.
ISBN 0-689-85159-6 (hardcover)
[1. Teeth—Fiction.
4. Humorous stori
Title.
PZ7.P1755
Sw 2005
[E]—dc21

first edition

Sweet Tooth

By Margie Palatini

Illustrated by Jack E. Davis

Simon & Schuster Books for Young Readers
New York   London   Toronto   Sydney

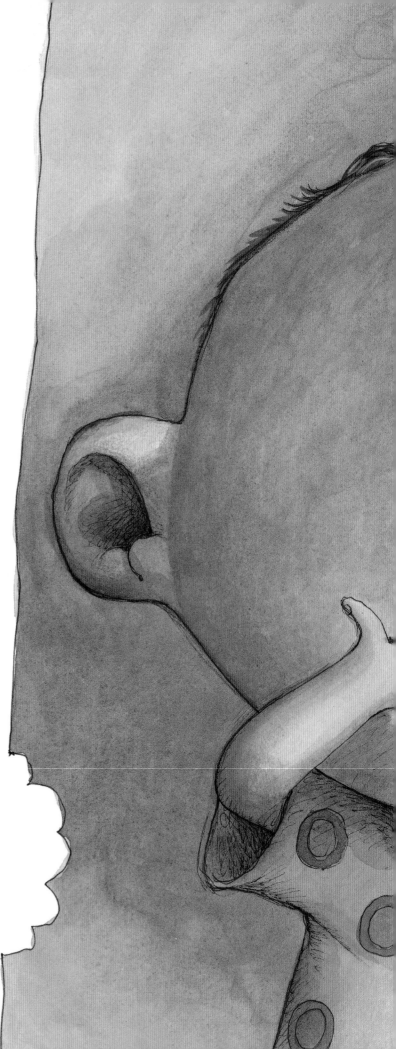

This is Stewart.

Your typical, average, everyday kid.

Except—for one thing.

"Iii oo-er ere."

Ahh, yes. There it is all right.

The molar in the back.

You're probably saying, "A tooth? What's the big deal about a tooth?"

And ordinarily you would be correct. . . . But that—is no ordinary tooth.

Uh-uh.

This is Stewart's sweet tooth. One nagging, annoying, demanding—

"BLAH. BLAH. BLAH. ENOUGH WITH THE YAKKIN'. I NEED A CANDY BAR. NOW-OW!"

—very loud, sweet tooth.

"DOES IT HAVE THAT GOOEY STUFF IN THE MIDDLE? 'CAUSE IT'S GOT TO HAVE THAT GOOEY STUFF IN THE MID-DLE!"

"There," said Stewart through a schmeared kisser and a gulp. "Satisfied?"

"AHHHHH . . . S-WEET!"

Yes, a tooth that wants what it wants, when it wants it . . . and lets everybody know it.

Take, for example, two years ago at cousin Charlotte's wedding. . . . Stewart was on his best behavior. His shoes were shined. Bowtie straight. Hands were spotless. Grandfather had just lifted his glass to toast the bride and groom when . . .

"I'm fallin' asleep here! Come on. Move it along, GRAMPS. Cut the cake. Time to cut the cake. I want the end hunk with all that iiiiii-icing."

"I don't know him," uttered Mother through a gritted smile.

"He doesn't belong to me," said Dad under his breath.

"Who is that boy?" muttered Grandmother.

Stewart wiped the pink rose from his lips. "It's The Sweet Tooth."

It was not a pretty picture.

The Tooth was no better behaved in school. Stewart had enough detention slips to wallpaper his room. Why, just two weeks ago . . .

"Who can tell me the capital of North Dakota?" asked Mrs. Finnegan in geography class.

"Jelly beans," said a muffled voice from the back of the room.

"Did you say something, Stewart?" asked Mrs. Finnegan.

"Licorice."

"Stewart, I'm afraid I can't hear your answer," said Mrs. Finnegan.

"Lollipops."

"You're going to have to speak up, Stewart."

"Hey! I'm dying here for a couple of CHOCOLATE PEANUT BUTTER CUPS, OKAY?!"

Detention slip number 432.

"But, I'm telling you, it's not me," said Stewart as he was led away to the principal's office. "It's The Tooth!"

The movies?

You don't really want to go there, do you? . . . Not with Stewart, anyway.

"Would somebody pass the yummy gummys, already?!"

"SHHHHHHHHHHHHH!"

"Don't look at me," chewed Stewart. "It's The Tooth."

And of course there was the unforgettable "Easter basket mishap."

Now that was really ugly.

That Sunday A.M. the family awoke to find jelly beans littering the living room. Marshmallow chicks were missing.

The trail of crumpled yellow foil wrappers led to one person, and one person only.

"Ooooh, Stewart," cried a disappointed Mother and Dad.

"I can't look," whimpered his sister, Allison, closing her eyes.

"Those chocolate bunnies never had a chance," moaned Stewart, rubbing his belly-aching stomach. "It was The Tooth."

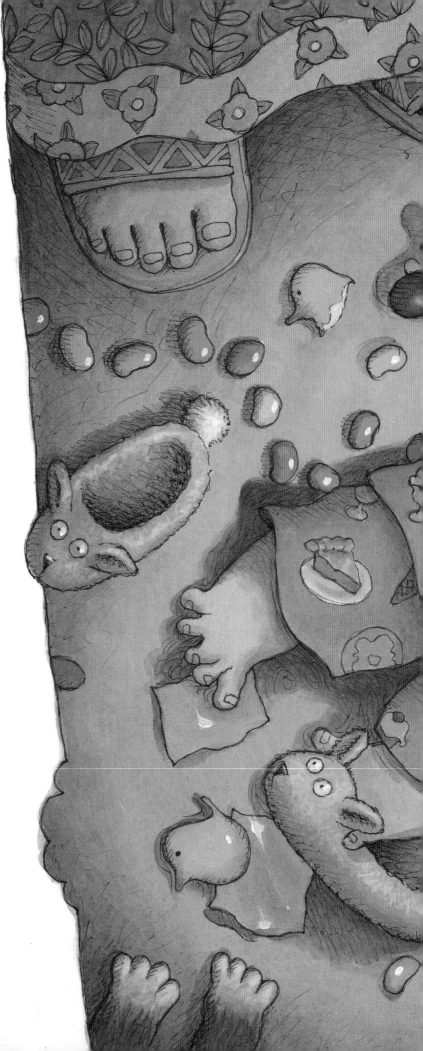

"HEY! CAN WE STOP GOING DOWN MEMORY LANE HERE AND OPEN UP THAT BAG OF COOKIES?"

"That's it. I've had enough!" cried Stewart.

"ENOUGH? I HAVEN'T EVEN HAD ONE."

"No more cookies!" shouted Stewart. "No more candy. No more cake. No more nothing!"

"That's no more anything," said The Tooth. **"And . . . WHO DO YOU THINK YOU'RE KIDDING, KID? Bring on those chocolate chips!"**

Stewart sighed.

What choice did he have? He was a boy with one big Sweet Tooth. He tore open the bag. He grabbed one, then two—three—four cookies. He opened his mouth.

"COME TO PAPA!" shouted The Tooth.

Stewart stopped.

"What are you waiting for, kid? Come on. Cookie. Cookie. Cookie. Cookie."

Stewart dropped the cookies.

But . . . not in his mouth.

"It's over, Tooth," said a suddenly determined Stewart. "I'm cutting you off. Starting right now. It's cold turkey."

"Cold turkey? Yee-ech! I hate cold turkey . . . unless you add a little cranberry sauce."

"Didn't you hear me, Tooth?" cried Stewart. "I said it's over. From now on there's nothing for you but a . . . a . . . a . . ." Stewart gulped. "Healthy diet."

"Healthy? Kid, say you don't mean it," wailed The Tooth.

But Stewart meant it, all right. He meant every word. Yes, it was trying. Yes, it was difficult. Okay, it was darn near impossible. But Stewart stayed strong.

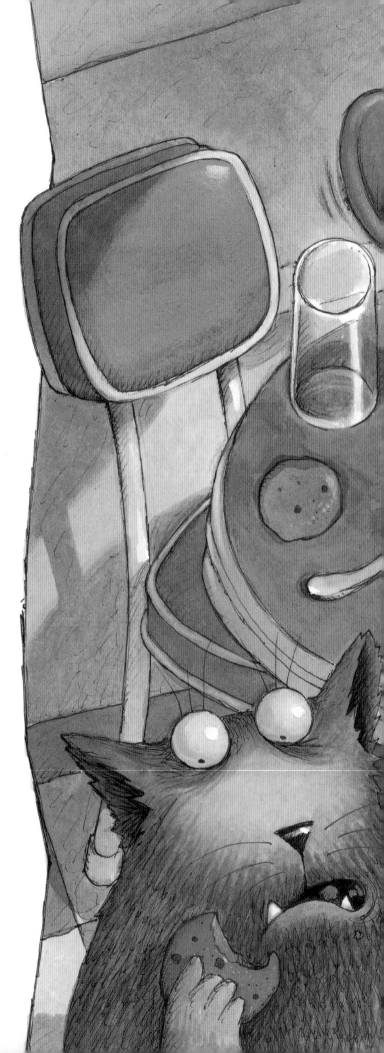

For The Tooth it was a different story.

"PEAS? YOU'RE GIVING ME PEAS? LITTLE DRY GREEN VEGGIE MARBLES? Broccoli? You're feeding me a shrub? THAT'S NOT GOING TO DO IT. DESSERT! WHERE'S DESSERT? I'm begging you. WHEN DO WE GET TO THE GOOD STUFF?"

"I can't hear you," said Stewart, putting down his fork and placing his hands over his ears. Strong. He stayed strong.

"Just one eensy-teensy CHOCOLATE-COVERED PEANUT before hitting the sack. How about it? . . . A nosh. A nibble. A breath mint. Somethin'!"

"Forget it," said Stewart, turning off the light. Strong. Strong.

"COME ON. WHADDAYA SAY? ONE SPOONFUL OF SUGAR," urged The Tooth as Stewart ate his cereal. Stewart shook his head.

The Tooth was losing its grip and it knew it. **"A DROP OF CHOCOLATE MILK. One measly little crumb-bun crumb."**

"No way," said Stewart. Very strong.

"HEY, WATCH THAT TOOTHBRUSH," shouted The Tooth. "AND KEEP THAT TONGUE OF YOURS ON THE OTHER SIDE OF YOUR MOUTH. TRYIN' TO WIGGLE ME OUT OF HERE, HUH? Well, I'm not going, kid. I'm not going anywhere! Do you hear me? . . . Do you hear me?"

Stewart brushed. Flossed. Gargled.

"U-u-ugh," moaned The Tooth, weakly. "He's not hearing me. . . . I'll get you for this, kid."

Stewart smiled. He was winning. Oh yes, he was winning.

Three days passed. The Tooth was quiet. Very quiet. Almost too quiet.

But Stewart wasn't thinking "tooth." He was thinking baseball.

It was the biggest game of the season. Bottom of the ninth. Stewart was at the plate. Runners were on second and third. Two outs. Two strikes.

The crowd was on their feet. The game was on the line. Stewart's team was down by one run. The pitcher went into his windup. There was a hush from the stands. A big fat fastball was heading for the plate. It was all up to Stewart. And then . . .

"BOY, COULD I GO FOR A HUNK OF BUBBLE GUM RIGHT NOW!"

Swing! Swish!

"Heh-heh-heh."

"Strike three!" yelled the umpire. "Y'er out!"

"Gotcha!" said The Tooth. **"Now go get me some goodies!"**

"I'll get you goodies," mumbled Stewart, dropping the bat.

Home he marched. Into the kitchen. Straight for the refrigerator. He yanked open the door. Rustled through the vegetable bin. He flung lettuce. He tossed tomatoes. He hurled a head of cauliflower. And then he pulled out—a carrot. That's right. A carrot.

"It's over for you, Tooth," announced Stewart defiantly, lifting the carrot above his head.

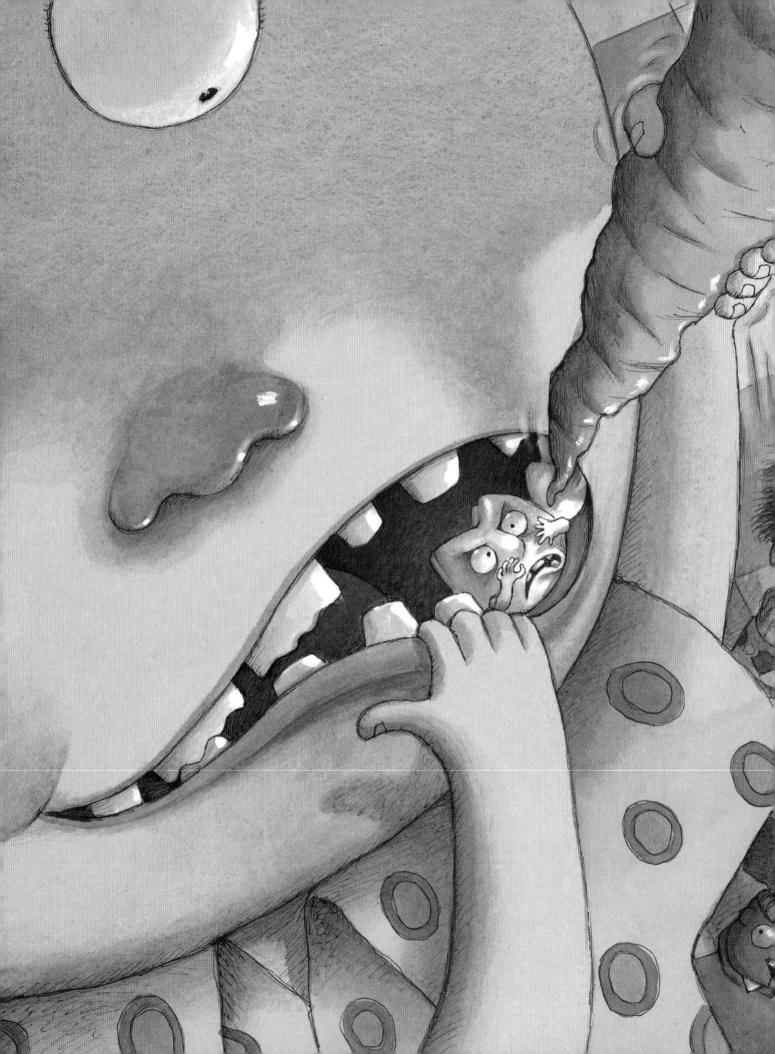

"What are you going to do with that?" asked his wide-eyed sister.

Stewart grinned. He opened his mouth wide. Very wide.

"KID! NO! NOT THE CARROT! NOT THE CARROT!"

"Yes. The carrot!" shouted Stewart.

"No, kid, no!"

Allison covered her eyes. "Am I too young to be watching this?"

Closer. Closer. Closer. And then—
CR-CR-CRUNCH.

"Ahhh-ahh-ahhhhh. . . . So long, sweet world! . . . What a way to go. . . . Done in by an orange veggie."

Stewart rubbed his jaw. He stared at the carrot . . . and The Tooth.

It was over.

"What's going to happen to it?" asked Allison as she followed her brother upstairs to the bedroom.

Stewart placed the molar under his pillow, then looked at his sister.

"Who knows?" he said with a big smile. "That's the tooth fairy's problem now."

"WAH, WAH, WAH!"
cried the baby teeth.

"WOOF!" yapped
the canine.

"Please be quiet,"
said the wisdom tooth,
"I'm trying to read."

**"Pipe down, wise
guy! What does a
sweet tooth have to
do to get an ice-
cream sundae
around here? With
hot fudge! And
throw some
sprinkles on it
while you're at it."**

The tooth fairy sighed.
"ROTTEN TEETH!"